Dedicated to all those who work tirelessly
for the cause of animal rights

Book design by Sue Redding and Sara Gillingham.
Typeset in Toronto Subway.
The illustrations in this book were rendered in Adobe Illustrator.
Manufactured in China.

Library of Congress Cataloging-in-Publication Data
Redding, Sue.
Up above and down below / by Sue Redding.
p. cm.
Summary: Illustrations and rhyming text reveal events happening in varied environments,
from an icy sea to a blistering desert, while very different things occur down below.
ISBN-13: 978-0-8118-4876-3 (13-digit)
ISBN-10: 0-8118-4876-0 (10-digit)
[1. Underground areas—Fiction. 2. Stories in rhyme.] I. Title.
PZ8.3.R2448Up 2006
[E]—dc22
2005013212

Distributed in Canada by Raincoast Books
9050 Shaughnessy Street, Vancouver, British Columbia V6P 6E5

10 9 8 7 6 5 4 3 2 1

Chronicle Books LLC
85 Second Street, San Francisco, California 94105

www.chroniclekids.com

uP aboVe

Sue Redding

& doWN beloW

chronicle books · san francisco

Early in the morning families buzz 'round the house,

while down in the cellar sleeps one tiny mouse.

While actors on stage are performing a play,

the crew down below is working away.

Ants march on a picnic and turn it upside down,

returning with treats for friends underground.

Fishermen fish among the penguins and seals.

unaware of the sights that the ice conceals.

As furry and feathered friends play up in the leaves,

creepy crawlies rule the ground underneath the trees.

As dogs and their owners stroll city streets,

people run for the train and rush to get to seats.

The desert is hot as the sun burns bright,

but way down below it's as cool as the night.

In a beautiful garden where vegetables grow,

rabbits pick veggies—shhh, the farmers don't know!

While sailors battle the dark stormy sea,

under the waves it's as calm as can be.

Golfers play with golf balls. Gophers do, too.

But they play with them differently than you and I do!

As passengers enjoy a cruise on the bay,

the crew below works hard throughout the day.

Up above and down below, under the moon's light,

parents hug children and kiss them goodnight.

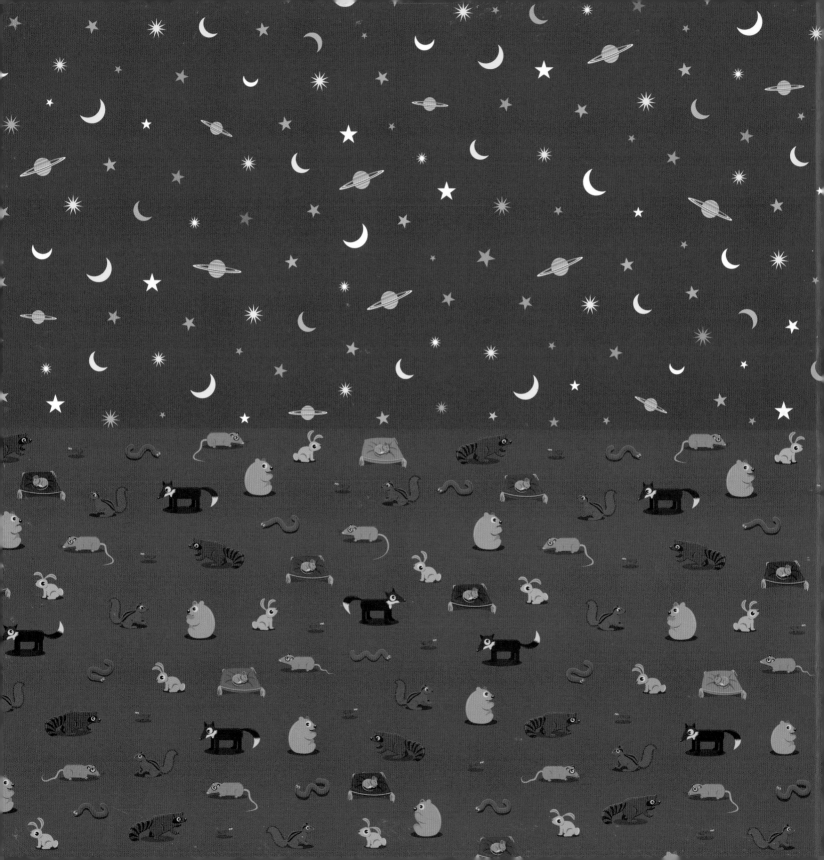